Only A Marquess Will Do

To Marry a Rogue, Book 4

COPYRIGHT

ONLY A MARQUESS WILL DO

TO MARRY A ROGUE, BOOK 4

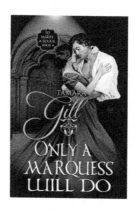

It's a game of instruction and seduction. But who's teaching who?

The London Season is not for Lady Victoria Worthingham. After a disastrous marriage that lasted no more than six weeks, she's sworn off men forever. But that doesn't mean she can't help her brother's best friend find his perfect match. It should be simple...unless she falls in love with him first, of course...

Marquess Albert Kester is everything ladies aren't looking for in a husband—socially awkward and bumbling as a debutante at her first ball. Writing adventures instead of living them seems to be his lot in life. Unless he can convince Victoria to stop seeing him as a project and start seeing him as a man, that is...

She's determined to see him happily settled. All he wants is her. Only one outcome is certain in this game.

Rules will be broken...and if they aren't careful, so will their hearts...

CHAPTER 1

London, 1809

*V*ictoria stood in the modiste on Bond street, the heat on her cheeks as warm as the day outdoors. She glanced about the room, the women of the ton, those who had the power to make or ruin a lady's chances during her Season, stared at her with pity—some with amusement and glee.

Her mother's mouth had not stopped gaping when her sister, Alice, now the Viscountess Arndel, had read the latest on dit in *The Times* that morning. That Victoria's husband, the very man she had married six weeks before, had run off with a maid at the estate.

Victoria stared down at the blue silk gown the modiste had halted pinning the hem for, her face too one of shock, but at least not glee. The modiste would know better than to find pleasure in such news with the daughter of a duke.

"I do not understand," her mama said, taking the newspaper from Alice and reading the article herself.

Victoria felt her cheeks heat with embarrassment. How could Paul do such a thing to her? She had thought they were happy, settled, and ready to start the next chapter of their lives. Only last week she had farewelled him when he went to check on his country estate. That this gossip rag all of London was devouring knew more about the state of her marriage than she did was mortifying. How could she have been so wrong about a person she cared for? She was never wrong.

"Pass me the paper, Mama." Her mother handed it over to her with haste, seemingly only too happy to have the offending article out of her hand. Victoria read the printed black letters, and with each word, her world crumbled about her.

It read: *"Mr. Paul Armstrong, the very one recently married to Lady Victoria Worthingham was seen sequestered at a local inn in Dover, the woman hanging off his every word most certainly not the Duke of Penworth's sister and new wife. That both Mr. Armstrong and his unnamed companion were soused, and too boisterous for the townsfolk was also mentioned. We can only look on Lady Victoria with pity over her most unhappy union that she so newly stepped into."*

She clamped her jaw shut, an expletive on the tip of her tongue. Paul was a wealthy landholder from Kent. A suitable gentleman for a woman such as herself. Her brother Josh, the Duke of Penworth assured her he was a good match, both financially and regarding the gentleman's reputation. When her brother returned from abroad, she would certainly have words with him regarding his character evaluations.

Not that their marriage was a love match, unlike her sisters who had found love with their spouses. But Victoria had never been one to think such a thing would happen to her. She was too opinionated, a little rough about the edges, blunt, and loved dogs and horses too much to be a diamond of the first water.

Where her sisters were refined and ladylike, she was, well, a little notched. A laugh caught her attention, and she looked over to find Miss Fanny Christi pointing and giggling over *The Times*. Victoria glared at the social-climbing ninny and thrust the paper aside, the modiste taking it without a word.

"I apologize for wasting your time with this gown, Mrs. DeRose, but it would seem that I'm no longer in the mood for a dress fitting." Victoria held out her arms. "Please help me to remove the gown. I shall return another day to complete the alterations."

"But dear, do you not want to write and demand Mr. Armstrong returns? The article could be incorrect. Why even now he could be on his way back from the country to explain this slanderous piece."

Victoria wiggled out of the gown, leaving her only in her shift as she stepped off the fitting stool in the store and went to change back into her morning dress. "It is not, Mama. Mr. Armstrong has made his choice." *And now he would have to live with it.* "I will not be one of those pitiful wives who allow such insults to stand. While I cannot change the fact that I am married, that does not mean I'll allow him to ruin my life. If it is freedom he wishes so soon after our nuptials, then I too shall live how I like and bedamn Paul to Hades."

Stupid fool to have ruined their future in such a way. Victoria walked into the change room, pulling the small curtain closed to hide her from those in the store who watched them and their reaction to the news like a kettle of vultures over a corpse.

Only then did she allow herself a deep breath, the reaction to the news that she had been hiding from all those prying eyes. She slumped onto the soft, padded chair in the stall. While she knew their marriage would have been a practical and good match, she had liked Paul, even if it were not a love match. He made her laugh and was handsome. She had thought they would muddle along well enough. His estate was large. He had a good stable of horses and was fond of dogs, had stated she could bring her two wolfhounds with her when they married, which she had.

She pulled her morning gown from the hook where it hung. She would not have minded had he wished to break the engagement, but to marry her and then run off? What had he been thinking! The stupid man could have been honest with her. Why did he not tell her the truth, that he loved another and did not wish to marry? That's if he loved the maid at all. For all she knew, perhaps this was the way the man truly was. A gentleman without honor.

Victoria stood and slipped the dress over her head, stepping back out into the store to gain assistance with the buttons on her back. Her mama handed her her bonnet and gloves, and within a few minutes, they were ready to leave.

"I'm so very sorry about your unsuccessful marriage, Lady Victoria," Miss Christi said, the smirk on her face telling Victoria that she was not sorry at all. "And so soon into the union. How you must be suffering."

Victoria looked down her nose at her, feeling the weight and support of both her mother and sister behind her. A duchess and viscountess who would never abide such rudeness for long, and neither would she.

Victoria patted Miss Christi's shoulder, hoping the condescension was thick and clear in her touch. "Do not be sorry for me, Miss Christi. It is not my loss, but my husband's." She smiled, glad to see Miss Christi's face had paled at her words. "I hope we see you at the ball this evening. It's always lovely to see off the Season with a bang."

Miss Christi curtsied to Victoria's mama while mumbling, "Of course. Good day, Your Grace, Lady Arndel."

Victoria turned up her nose and left the store. Their coachman opened the door and helped them inside. Victoria heard her mama tell the driver they were for home, and it wasn't long before the carriage wheels were rumbling over the gravel and cobblestone roads through Mayfair.

No one spoke, all of them too disturbed by what had just transpired, no matter how it may have looked to those who viewed them in the store.

"Well, I hope Mr. Armstrong is pleased with his actions. I shall endeavor never to allow him to step foot in any of our entertainments in the future or those of my children. He is cut off from our family. Dead to us all I swear."

Alice nodded, her lips thinning in displeasure. "You should not allow him to get away with such treatment, Victoria. We ought to pay him back in some way. I could always shoot him. My aim is second to none as you know."

Victoria glanced at her sister, unsure how much help Alice would be since she was in the early stages of pregnancy. "I think Callum may take issue with me having you hie about England searching for a man who does not want to be found and shooting him. Not yet, at least." Victoria stared out onto the street, not really seeing anything other than a city she would be happy to leave. Next week, in fact, she was due to return to Paul's country estate where they were to remain until next Season. That would not be happening now.

What a waste of effort these past months had been. The courtship, the marriage, the expense. Victoria supposed she should feel more upset than she did, but she couldn't bring forth the emotions to do so. That in itself told her that to lose her husband, while humiliating, was not life-ending.

She would clasp the opportunity his foolishness had gifted her and return to Dunsleigh.

"You may do whatever you think is best, Mama. I, for one, will hold my head high at tonight's ball, and next week we shall return home and go on with things as if nothing has happened." Victoria leaned forward, taking her mama's hands. "Do not think that I am so very upset, for I am not. In fact," she said, leaning against the squabs, "I'm certain since he's decided to run off with a maid, society will punish him enough without me adding to his woes. But as for our marriage, it is over and nothing, no persuasion from him in the future will change my mind. As far as I am concerned, I will view myself as a widow from this day forward."

"I think you may be right," Alice said, rubbing her small baby bump. "You are destined for better things, my dearest. Who is attending this evening, Mama? We need to show society that we have rallied around Victoria and will not abide her being slighted."

"Well, as for that," her mama said, rattling off several families, all of whom Victoria knew and classed as friends. They would not offend or slight her in her time of need. They would be home soon. Safe from London and the gossiping ton.

While she did not know what her future held, where she would live, or what name to use, one thing she was at least grateful for... Her dowry was still her own, and no matter where Paul traveled with his lover, he could not swindle her money away. She supposed she could purchase a townhouse in London or a small country estate near Dunsleigh. All ideas would need considerable thought and once they were home, she would be able to set her mind to figuring out her future.

One thing was certain however, her future would not involve her husband. Not ever again.

Hampshire, 1811

*A*lbert Kester, Marquess Melvin wrote the final words in his latest gothic romance novel. His quill scrawled *The End*—a little salute to himself he always signed when he'd completed a manuscript.

He leaned back in his chair, staring out at the inky-black night. Secluded away in Hampshire near Surrey's border, he ought to feel alone, vulnerable perhaps, and yet, he did not.

He loved living in the country. The hunting lodge he now used as his writing oasis was the perfect setting for a man such as himself, a man who did not enjoy crowds or socializing. He'd never been one to have the abilities to speak pretty to females or act as one of the rogues, gambling and carousing about the town without a care.

But he would have to soon. In a week or so, his closest neighbor and influential family were returning to Surrey, and he would have to ride the ten miles between their estates and endure the weekend house party and ball the Duke of Penworth held.

And he would see her again...

Lady Victoria Worthingham, now widow to the late Mr. Paul Armstrong after the fool dabbled with the wrong married lady abroad and received a bullet through his skull for his troubles. The only woman he was certain of in England and perhaps the world to make him question his life. His way of living. So private and alone.

The invitation had arrived today, and he'd sent off an acceptance without delay before he could change his mind and remain at Rosedale.

Albert slipped the manuscript into the leather binder he used and locked the book away in a cabinet before securing the lodge and returning to the main house.

He had not brought his horse this afternoon, knowing he

would be several hours here, but it did not matter. He knew his way back home, even in the night.

At least he could attend the ball at the duke's estate without the nagging guilt he always suffered when he had a book due. With it finished, he could at least attempt to enjoy the ball more.

The lights to the main house flickered through the trees and then rose high before him as he cleared the copse of forest that surrounded his estate. Tomorrow he would send his book off to his publisher and, should they like the next installment of his series, his book would be available within the next twelve months or so.

It may not be the usual occupation that a marquess would do, but he enjoyed writing stories, becoming lost in his characters' worlds. What started as a hobby was now another source of income to his estate, and it pleased him. He could control that world. He could not control the one he lived in.

His mother, who resided on an estate just outside of Bath with her new husband, was forever writing to him, asking when he would return to London for another Season. Find a bride to marry and have an heir. A grandchild she longed for.

He knew his mama had a lot of love to give. His father had been a cruel man, a bullying bastard, and all the love she had for the man withered and died only years into the marriage. Now she was happy. They both were, he supposed, in their small, different ways, but she wanted to share the love she had bottled up for so many years.

Albert, too, would like to love. He would like to court Lady Victoria, but since the scandal of her husband's affair, his running off with a maid followed by several other indiscretions all written about in the London gossip rags, Victoria looked less than interested in entering such a union for a second time.

Who could blame her for such thoughts.

While he liked the idea of marriage, he certainly had no idea what to do with a wife once the union was officiated. A problem he'd been trying to solve with extensive research. He'd purchased a collection of books on the art of lovemaking, sketches of how it was that women and men came together—drawings depicting the act of lovemaking, some of which had taken his breath away.

Albert let himself into the house, his staff well used to the strange times he came and went. He walked into the library and went directly to the latest book he had received from London about the life story of Moll Flanders, having left it on his desk before he'd set off to write this afternoon. An amusing and interesting account, with some bawdy tales that entertained him.

With his books featuring scenes similar to those he found in Daniel Defoe's book, he hoped he at least sounded as true and accurate as this author. His career would be over should the public know the truth. That one of their favorite gothic romance authors who pens tales of intrigue, horror, and passionate encounters was as virginal as a debutante newly arrived in London. A marquess, too, even more humiliating. Lords ought to know how to romance a lady or rake about town.

He was living a lie, at least portraying one. But then, he supposed his books were a work of fiction, and his characters had nothing to prove. But soon, he would need to search for a wife in earnest. Court her, as awkward and clumsy as he was when in verbal conversation with females. The thought made him frown. Next week he would see Lady Victoria, and his ineptitude would be even more noticeable. Her vivaciousness for life, her confidence shamed his introverted self. For years he had wanted the gumption to implement some of the things he'd found in the sketches with her, seduce her into marriage with him.

A dream that was unlikely to come true. He required a wife who at least wished for a husband. Lady Victoria Worthingham, as much as he longed for the position to be filled by her, was the one woman in England sworn off ever marrying again. Everyone knew it, and so did he. Someone else would have to do.

CHAPTER 2

Dunsleigh, 1811

*T*he guests to their country ball and short house party arrived a week after the 1811 Season had come to an end. After their return, Victoria had the following day walked up to the family mausoleum and paid her respects to her papa, a man she missed more with each passing year, especially when she saw all that he missed by being gone. The many grandchildren being born, the happy marriages, the balls, and parties that she knew he loved so very much.

Tonight was the formal dinner the night before the ball, where the guests could relax and enjoy a more intimate get together after their journeys to Surrey. There would be music and games, cards for the gentlemen, and of course, the guests could stroll the extensive grounds, or enjoy the billiards room or conservatory if they chose.

It seemed all of London had descended on Dunsleigh for the ball, including a lot of the local gentry, some of whom rarely went up to London at all.

TAMARA GILL

Lord Melvin one of them. After dinner, Victoria stood beside Alice, discussing those who were in attendance. Her sister was positively glowing with a second pregnancy in as many years, and Callum, her adoring husband, kept vigil from across the room, speaking to her two brothers-in-law, the Earl of Muir and the Duke of Moore.

"What do you think of Lord Melvin? He does seem most uncomfortable with Miss Fletcher, do you not think? Why," Victoria said, sipping her ratafia with amusement, "I do believe he is sweating. Look." She shook Alice's arm a little.

Her sister cast a cursory glance, not wanting to be too obvious in their appraisal of him. "Oh dear, he's pulling at his cravat. What do you think Miss Fletcher has said to him to make him so uncomfortable?

Something about the gentleman had always drawn Victoria. She supposed as a lover of animals, of dogs especially and horses, to see a man who looked as downtrodden and as uncomfortable as a puppy surrounded by wolves would make one feel bad for the man.

Feel sorry for the unfortunate.

As one of her brother's closest friends since school, they knew him well, and for many years. In the two years since she'd seen him last, his lordship appeared even more uneasy around company. As if society made him physically ill.

She cringed when he fumbled for his handkerchief and dabbed at his brow. "He's nervous. Maybe he likes Miss Fletcher."

Victoria narrowed her eyes at the idea of Lord Melvin seeking to court the young heiress. From the way Miss Fletcher controlled the narrative of their conversation, she couldn't help but think the poor man would never get a word in.

But then he probably wouldn't get a word in with her either,

12

so there was that. Even so, as she studied him, she couldn't help but think he'd like to bolt like one of her mares when let out of the stables after a few days. "Do you think I should save him and pull Miss Fletcher away for a turn about the room?"

Alice cast her a cursory glance. "Why the interest in Lord Melvin?" She tipped her head to the side, regarding the gentleman. "I suppose he is quite sweet-looking. A little bookish perhaps, but that is nothing if he has other skills."

Victoria snorted and covered her inappropriate lapse of ladylike manners by covering her mouth with her hand. She took several moments to stop chuckling. "I'm not even going to ask what you mean by that, Alice. But let me enlighten you, dear sister. I have seen you and your husband when you think you're alone, and so I can assume very well what 'skills' you mean."

Alice did not bat an eyelash, nor did she blush. She simply grinned, sipping her wine. "I suppose what one does not know can be taught. Myself included. I was quite enlightened after marrying Callum."

"And what are we to do should both the couples be clue-less?" Not that she was or that she thought Lord Melvin would be so very naïve when it came to seduction and women. He was a man, after all. A marquess. He could not have been so secluded and innocent, no matter if he spent all of his time in the country. He probably had a gaggle of women willing and able to warm his bed in Hampshire.

She narrowed her eyes at the thought. At that very moment, his lordship glanced away from Miss Fletcher, his attention colliding with hers. The fear, the uncomfortable mess he was just an instant before vanished, and a deter-mined light entered his eyes that she'd never seen before. What did that mean?

Alice cleared her throat, grinning over the top of her

crystal glass. "Well, well, well, he certainly looks a lot more dashing when he sees you. I wonder...".

Victoria moved her attention on to the dancers, feigning interest in them instead. "Do not be asinine, Alice. I'm not the least interested in Lord Melvin and nor is he in me."

"I believe the same may not be said for his lordship."

"What about a certain lordship?" their older sister Elizabeth, Countess Muir, asked, joining them and kissing them both in turn on their cheeks.

Victoria clasped her sister's arm, having not seen her for several months since they resided most of the time at Muirdeen, their Scottish estate.

Alice nodded in Lord Melvin's direction. "Victoria has sparked the interest of a certain marquess. Although instead of a rogue, which I'm sure you would agree with me make the best husbands, he seems more righteous."

Elizabeth grinned at Victoria. "There is nothing wrong with righteousness. Henry wasn't a rogue, far from it, and he's simply delightful to be married to."

"That is true, and really, I suppose Callum wasn't either. Not a rascal one in any case. So there may be hope for our Lord Melvin after all."

Victoria stepped away from her sisters, pinning them with disapproving glares. "You forget my husband was the worst of men. Whoring his way around England and the continent. There is no 'our Lord Melvin,' and you must stop saying such things. I noticed his unease and merely commented on it. You're reading too much into my observations."

Elizabeth tossed Alice a knowing smile. "Of course, dearest, but that does not mean all men are the same," she said, her voice cajoling.

"I'm going to find Isolde. You two are impossible." Victoria strode off, locating Isolde beside her mama. Her sister's husband—who doted on his wife to the point of nauseating regularity—winked at Victoria when she came up to them. She bussed his cheek and then her sister's. "We need to disown our other two sisters, they're impossible."

Their mother raised her brow, looking over to where Alice and Elizabeth talked and laughed amongst themselves. "What have they done to you, dearest? Do you wish for me to speak to them?"

Victoria shook her head, knowing her grievances with her siblings weren't so very bad. That they teased her over a man she herself was curious about did not help. She didn't like everyone knowing her secrets. She had not thought mentioning Lord Melvin's unease would cause such curiosity. Or the fact of seeing him with a woman would disarm her so very much. After the death of her husband, she had promised herself a life of doing whatever she wished. No more husbands to make fools of their wives. The desire to travel and a life of adventure awaited her. Having children and a spouse did not.

"It is nothing, Mama. Do not trouble yourself."

Her mama studied her a moment before one of her friends waved her over to join them and she excused herself.

"Tell me you're staying at Dunsleigh for several weeks. I do not think I can stand being here with only Alice as a neighbor to keep me company."

The disappointment on Isolde's face told Victoria that she was not staying long. "We are for home next week, my love. But you may come with us if you like. We should love to have you if you wished for a little diversion. Wiltshire is very lovely this time of year."

"I best stay with mama. She'll be alone here should I go anywhere, and with Josh abroad, I had better not go too far away. But thank you, maybe Mama and I can both come and see you for a week or two before Christmas."

"That would be lovely," Isolde said.

Happy with this plan, Victoria spoke to guests as they socialized about the room. The evening was a success and in full swing by the time supper was served. Victoria stood at the threshold of the supper room doors, content to watch those who were hungry eating. She reached up and massaged her nape when a prickling of awareness skittered across her skin.

She turned and found Lord Melvin several paces behind her. His unease at the crowded supper room visible on his pinched features. Victoria took pity on the man, going into the room and picking several favorite dishes of hers before quitting the space.

"Lord Melvin, how good to see you tonight. I have some supper for you if you would like a repast."

He gazed down at the plate of food, and it seemed to break the spell of inactivity that plagued him. "Oh, Lady Victoria, I thank you. You did not have to do such a service for me."

"I'm a hostess here this evening with my mama, my lord. It is only right that each of our guests is cared for."

He took the plate, his fingers grazing hers at the interchange, and Victoria started at the feel of his gloved fingers against hers. He was warm, with strong hands that made her feel a little odd. A little too curious for her liking.

"It's crab cakes and lobster in jelly. They're my first choice at any ball. I hope you like them."

His lips tilted into a half smile. Victoria sensed that when relaxed, this man would open up like a flower. Not that she viewed most men as plants, but with her at least, right now, the fear that lurked in his dark-blue orbs had dissipated.

"I do thank you," he said again.

She stayed with him with nowhere else to be for a time, content to wait for supper to end and the dancing to begin again. "I have not seen you tread the ballroom floor this evening. Do you not like to dance, my lord?" she asked him.

He chewed and swallowed one of his crab cakes before answering, "I do enjoy dancing, and if you are not otherwise engaged, would you dance the next set with me?"

"The next set is to open with a waltz. Do you waltz too, my lord?"

"I have been known to on occasion," he drawled, his voice dropping to a deep, husky purr that she did not think him capable of. Not with his nervousness that plagued him. The man was so very curious. A sense of anticipation thrummed down her spine, and she liked the idea of being in his arms. "Then the dance is yours, my lord. Come find me when you have finished your supper." Would he falter or endure? Something told Victoria she was about to find out.

CHAPTER 3

*B*y the time supper had ended and the musicians set up for the commencement of the next set, Albert had all but lost his nerve. It was one thing to invite a woman out to dance, but it was quite another to follow through with the act.

What if he stumbled and fell, pulled Lady Victoria down with him? What if he grew more nervous than he already was and sweated profusely? The idea of stepping on her toes, hurting her delicate feet was beyond reprehensible and unforgivable.

She would never dance with him again, and he wanted her to dance with him, especially now. Now that she was out of mourning for her husband. The fool Armstrong had lost a prize when he tossed Lady Victoria over for a maid not long after their marriage. Whatever was the man thinking! Albert certainly did not know or understand such motives.

He would never throw her over for anyone else. How could he, she was perfection personified.

Like an angel, she materialized before him, holding out

her hand, a mischievous light in her eyes. "Our dance, I believe, Lord Melvin."

He led her out onto the floor, hoping his nervousness did not shine through. Women in general made him fumble like a fool, but Victoria more so than any. He didn't want her to view him as some simpleton. He wanted her to view him as so much more.

Like a gentleman. A man.

Albert pulled her into his arms as the music commenced. She was tall for a woman. Her eyes level with his chin. Her body was soft, womanly, and his, for a little time at least.

She smelled divine, like jasmine and soap. Never had he ever smelled something so sweet before. Her fingers flexed on his shoulder, and she looked up to meet his gaze. "I do believe this is our first dance, my lord."

How he wished it were more than that pitiful number. Albert had longed to ask her during the seasons he traveled to town to step out with him. He had wanted to have her in his arms more times than he could count, but his nerves never allowed him to speak the words necessary.

He wasn't sure why he was the way he was, and as much as he tried to hide his anxieties from the ton, they were always there, beneath his skin and threatening to make him miss out on life.

He supposed maybe his father's mistreatment of his family had something to do with it.

"We missed you this Season in town, my lord. Do say you're to attend next year."

He glanced down and met Lady Victoria's eyes. She was always so genuine and kind. Was it wishful thinking on his behalf that she would look at him more than a friend? If she gave him a chance to prove himself, he would not let her down.

Not an easy conquest when she was determined never to marry again, or so the gossips tittered behind their fans.

"I may attend. Will you be there, my lady, or has a gentleman now won your heart, and you're to be married?" Albert wasn't sure where the words came from, inappropriate and rude. He frowned, wishing he had a filter on his mouth at times. If he could have smacked himself about the head, he would have, knowing she wasn't long out of mourning.

Victoria laughed, easing a little of his tension. "No, I'm not engaged as I'm certain you already know. I'm home at Dunsleigh for the foreseeable future, until my brother returns home and helps me with my travels abroad. My sister is in a delicate state yet again you see, and I wish to be close to her. Josh will return from abroad before Christmas so it will be a jolly good time here. One that is sorely needed after the past two years we have endured."

Albert understood her words but did not pry any further. The scandal her husband caused, the pain and embarrassment she must have withstood would have been enough to cripple him in society permanently. And yet, here she was, rising from the ashes like the strong, capable woman he knew her to be. How fortunate she was to have a supportive family. Other than his mama, there was no one else he could turn to, but a distant cousin he hardly knew. His father had passed, and he had no siblings.

It was no wonder people concerned him so much. He wasn't used to them.

"I shall like to see Penworth again. It has been almost a year."

"Yes, by the time Josh returns home, he would have been away that long. We're all so very excited to see him again." She looked up at him, her eyes wide and clear and direct. Always with the ability to pin someone to the ground with one look. "I forget you are friends with Josh. He has so many, but you were very close once. Still are, I hope."

They were still close. He received a monthly letter from the duke, one person other than Victoria he was calm around. Not that he was so very calm around Victoria right at this moment. Having her in his arms made him want things he'd never imagined before.

His gaze dipped to her lips, and he watched as she spoke of this and that, the ball and the guests, the food, and how late the night would be. All the while, all he could think about was if the pink, pouty flesh of her lips was as soft as it looked.

With some alarm, he realized she had stopped speaking and was staring at his mouth as well. Her tongue flicked out, licking her lips, and his body grew taut.

He read the question in hers, surprise even. Albert cleared his throat, breaking the spell between them. "With you home and Penworth due to return, may I invite you all over for dinner one evening at Rosedale? I admit my staff and their exemplary cooking abilities are poorly underutilized."

She smiled, and the action made her appear more beautiful than she already was. Albert had always thought Victoria the prettiest of the Worthingham sisters, tall and bold, but also caring even though he suspected very few other than her family knew how kind she was.

She certainly always took pity on him, made him feel welcome. A marquess or not, that wasn't something every one of his acquaintances fulfilled.

"I do not believe I've ever been to your estate, my lord. I understand Rosedale is very beautiful."

Not as beautiful as you, he wanted to say. If he were a rogue, had the ability for pretty words and dark, hungry looks, he would tell Victoria all those things. Instead, he masked his feelings and said, "One of the finest in Hampshire. Although I'm very close to Surrey and it is often contested which county I live."

"We would love to attend and be your guests, but I must say, and please forgive my forwardness, but may we stay a night? I know it is some miles from Dunsleigh and may be too great a distance to travel in one day."

"Oh, of course. You are more than welcome to stay." The idea of Victoria being in his home, asleep under the same roof, where he would be even more at ease, able to speak to her without the worry of prying eyes was just the thing. If he studied up on his books regarding the opposite sex and what was expected of him as a man, maybe he could prove to Victoria that he was worth more than friendship.

That he was worth her giving up her widowhood to marry him instead.

"Then we shall come as soon as Josh has returned, and you write and invite us." The strains to the waltz started to come to a regretful end. Albert did not want to let her go, but then he had two other dancers with her yet, but both would not allow him such close intercourse.

The evening passed pleasantly after his dances with Victoria, and he was content to stand by and watch the play of guests. Some hours later, he left the ball, asking permission for the use of the library. Thankfully the duchess did not ask as to why he wanted to use the room. A little while later, he was scribbling away his words on a new book, the heroine, as all of his were, remarkably similar to Victoria in both appearance and temperament.

He wrote for hours, the sounds of the music drifting to a close, just as the ball did as well. The first signs of the new day broke across the land, and the house started to wake with the whispered words of maids and footmen. Albert wet his forefinger and snuffed his candle. He leaned back in the chair, stretching. He wrote a good amount of the book last evening, a scene where the hero required saving. His heroine coming to the hero's rescue. He did not like weak characters and rarely wrote them. He supposed because he was that very thing in a lot of ways. Awkward, sheltered, and not the least fashionable. A weak marquess just as his father had always called him.

He collected his papers, placing them in his leather folder, and left the library. The guests wouldn't be up for some hours, and so he would rest and then say his goodbyes this afternoon before heading back to Rosedale, living in the hope that Victoria would do as she said and come to stay. The time would allow him to become worldly, a gentleman worthy of her hand, the hand of a daughter and sister to a duke.

CHAPTER 4

*V*ictoria stumbled into the library just as the day after the ball was almost at an end. The previous night had been amusing and enjoyable, but she would be happy when the Season would be officially over, and Dunsleigh would be just for her family and herself to enjoy.

Some of the guests had departed early, one of them Lord Melvin, whom she had seen off just after lunch. She walked to the desk, needing some parchment to write to her brother, when she spotted a piece of paper, the scribbly, messy writing bold and rushed as if someone had to get the words down quickly before they forgot them.

She picked up the paper, reading the words, and couldn't quite grasp what she was holding. A marvelous story, similar in tone and ability to others she had read by one of her favorite authors, Elbert Retsek. His aptitude to throw the reader into his gothic romances was something of a dream. She had often fantasized about meeting the gentleman, having him sign the many books she had of his. In fact, she was eagerly awaiting his next release, which was rumored to be coming out next year.

She read through the words quickly, unable to comprehend how it was that these words were here. Was Elbert a guest at their home? She sat on the chair, reaching for the list of guests her mama had been checking and double-checking this past week.

She followed each guest's name, scrolling with her finger, and could not see anyone of that name on the list. Victoria frowned, slumping back in the chair. Was Elbert Retsek an alias, a pseudonym? How astonishing if he was a guest. Had she danced with him? Had she unknowingly been in the hands of one of England's up-and-coming writers, in the league of Horace Walpose or even Ann Radcliffe? Excitement thrummed through her veins at the idea of a real-life author being in their presence.

Alice strolled into the room and, spotting her, shut the door. "Ah, there you are. I wanted to come and see you before we returned home."

Victoria waved her sister over, and she quickened her steps. "Look and read this. I think it may be some pages from Elbert Retsek."

Alice frowned, taking the sample and reading it quickly. She pursed her lips. "Well, it certainly reads like him, but what is it doing here?"

"I came in here this morning," Victoria said, standing and smoothing her dress as she paced back and forth to the window, "and found it. I think he may have been a guest at the ball last evening and left this here by mistake." *Oh dear, which means he is missing an important piece of his story, for it looked like the hero was in great danger, not that she seemed too worried about the fact.* A point for why Victoria loved Elbert's stories so much. She hated weak characters in any story being outsmarted or, worse, killed.

"He'll be wanting it back then," Alice said, sitting at the desk. "What shall we do?"

Victoria made a point of looking at Alice's baby belly. "We will do nothing, but I shall. I will have to do some investigating."

"Hmm," Alice said, staring at her. "Oh, I know what you can do. Check the acceptances for the ball. Maybe your mystery guest replied himself, and the handwriting may be similar."

Hope rushed through Victoria. "Alice, that is brilliant. I shall do that straightaway." Not that she was an expert at comparing handwriting, but it was at least one way forward. What would she do when she found the gentleman who had attended? She wasn't sure. How does one approach a famous, if not closeted, author and tell them you knew who they were and that they had left part of their manuscript in one's library? He may be unsettled knowing that one of his own class knew of his profession. Not that she would ever tell a soul, not if that is what he wished. To remain anonymous would be his choice, and she would respect that.

Victoria strode over to the sideboard and opened the drawer. It was where her mama kept her invitations and responses for the current entertainments. She found the acceptances and picked them up, not willing to let them out of her sight. "I shall take these to my room and go through them. I should think it will take me several hours."

"Do come and see me when you think you've found a match. I would like to help you if I can. You know how much I love a good intrigue."

Victoria chuckled, remembering the many intrigues her sister landed herself in while being courted by Lord Arndel. Many of which Victoria was dragged into and made an accessory.

"I will, I promise." Victoria helped her sister stand and walked her to the door, bussing her cheeks before seeing her off with her husband.

Her mama came to stand beside her, waving off her daughter, and Victoria linked arms with her parent. "Only a few more guests to go, and we shall have our house to ourselves again."

Her mother led her back inside, a small smile playing about her mouth. Her mama was still a beautiful woman for her middle age, and since their father had died, had become a lot less strict with rules and etiquette. She was more carefree, let her children live the lives they wished, within reason, and be happy. Victoria wasn't sure why their mama had mellowed. Perhaps it simply came with age.

"Did you enjoy yourself last night, my dear? From what Lucy told me this morning, you were up all night dancing."

That was true. She had stayed at the ball longer than she normally would, but then, it was a send-off to the Season, and now she could enjoy riding about the estate, looking after her dogs. Some, she knew, spoke about her behind her back, snarled that she did not mourn her husband respect-fully enough, but she had. She had spent a year mourning a man who had not shown an ounce of honor during their six-week marriage. That society would judge her for his actions irked. It was one of the reasons she wanted to throw their ideals in their faces and remain a contented widow for the rest of her life.

"It was very enjoyable. Several gentlemen asked me to dance, which was nice of them, " she lied to keep her mama happy. "I was able to catch up with several friends, some of whom I shall not see again until next year."

Her mother chuckled, her eyes bright with amusement. "I shall live in the hope that the right gentleman is out there for you, my dear. You cannot allow what Mr. Armstrong put you through to tarnish your opinion on marriage."

Too late for that...

"Just so," Victoria said. "In fact, I wanted to let you know that I have borrowed the acceptances from the ball. I want to match up some writing samples if I can."

They walked up the stairs and into her mama's private parlor, where they would not be interrupted by other guests still staying at the house. "Really, why would you need to do that?" Her mother pulled the bell for tea. "Did a gentleman leave you an inappropriate note to rendevous with him? As a widow, you must protect yourself against such rakes."

Heat kissed Victoria's cheeks, although the idea of a wicked rendevous with a willing gentleman may not be so bad. One thing she would give Paul credit for was his bedroom abilities, and she had enjoyed the short time they had been together. Even if the idea of him with other women now soured that memory. "Of course not. You should know very well that is quite inappropriate. I would not think anyone would dare to try such things with Josh watching my every step. I do believe he still thinks me an unmarried maid."

Her mother raised one disbelieving brow. "Josh darling is not here to keep vigil. I would think many gentlemen would try such tricks. You're a beautiful woman, an heiress, and a widow."

"Well, that is not why I'm researching penmanship, Mama. I found a written page on the desk in the library and merely wanted to return it to its owner. After reading it, I should imagine it's quite important."

Having sat and picked up her sewing, her mother looked up at Victoria at her last words. "A note, you say? Left on the desk in the library overnight?"

"Yes," Victoria stated, her stomach a little in knots seeing her mother mull over the issue.

"You do not need to search the acceptances, my dear. I know who worked in the library last evening, as he sought my approval before doing so."

Victoria tried to school her features. Her mama had never been too accepting of her reading gothic romances or horror, and to find out that one of her guests could be England's latest on dit and had used the desk would never do. She would be scandalized.

"Who was it?" she asked in the most bored tone she could muster.

Her mama threaded a needle, her mouth pinched in concentration. "Lord Melvin requested use of the room late in the evening. He said he has some correspondence to finish."

Lord Melvin!

"Do close your mouth, dear. You're gaping."

Victoria shut her mouth with a snap. Lord Melvin? How could it be him!? He was so quiet, and some would say a little droll, but handsome, so handsome that every time she saw him, a little devil sat on her shoulder, and she wanted to tease him, not that she ever did. Last evening he had invited her family and herself to his estate. Could she wait until then to confront him with this idea of hers?

His written words, folded and safe in the pocket of her dress, weighed heavily on her conscience. No, she could not wait. He may need this part of his story. If she did not return it to him, he would wonder what happened to it. He would have to rewrite it.

The horror!

She was not a writer, but to think of losing any part of a manuscript would surely send fear to shiver down one's spine.

"That reminds me, Mama. Lord Melvin invited us to stay at Rosedale when Josh has returned from abroad."

"Oh, did I not tell you, my dear? Josh darling will be home next week. I received a letter from him this morning. He's in

Paris right now but will start his movement back to England within a day or two."

What wonderful news. Her trip to Hampshire could be sooner than she thought. "Do you think Josh would agree to travel and stay at Lord Melvin's so soon after returning from abroad?"

Her mother set down her sewing, meeting her gaze. "I do not see why not. The Season is over, and we're now rusticating in the country for several months. I'm sure he will agree."

Victoria flopped herself down on a nearby settee. And if she were to hint to Josh that Lord Melvin may be a possible suiter, she was certain he'd have them bundled up in the carriage within the hour. Not that she was looking at his lordship as a possible match, but she was certainly curious about this story she had in her pocket. Had he written it? Was he the mysterious Elbert Retsek the whole of England was talking about? Victoria crossed her legs, grinning. Something told her he was, and what a find that shall be. What would he have to say for himself about his double life in society?

Only time would tell.

CHAPTER 5

*A*s expected, her brother rumbled up the drive in the duke's carriage several days later. Victoria and her mama went out the front of the house to greet him. The carriage was sprayed with mud, and the two drivers and footmen accompanying Josh looked tired and worn.

Victoria turned to the housekeeper standing behind her and requested a light repast and drinks for the travel-weary duke and servants.

Josh jumped down from the carriage, and Victoria hardly recognized him. Gone was the boy they had always teased growing up. The only boy in the family, it was only right that he suffered a little bit. Not that they were ever cruel, but he had been the future duke, and it was always fun to remind him that although he would care for them all one day, he was still the youngest.

Victoria ran up to him, wrapping her arms around his waist, hugging him. "You're home. Finally."

He kissed the top of her head, pulling their mama into his arms as she joined them. They walked inside, arms linked. They were a close family, and she knew that Alice would be around later today when she received word he was home. Isolde and Elizabeth had returned to their estates, but Josh would undoubtedly visit with them soon enough.

"Ah, Dunsleigh. How I have missed our home and everyone in it. Tell me all that has happened while I was away." Josh turned and looked down at her, and Victoria marveled at how much of a man he appeared. He was taller, broader across the shoulders, his hair lightened by travel and a little too long for what was fashionable. His eyes were bright and merry, and he required a shave, his whiskers a little too long.

Had the ladies in London seen him this past Season, Victoria knew he would have been swamped. How fun next year would be when he returned to town.

"I see that you are not yet married," he teased, bussing the top of her head again as they stepped into the foyer. "Remind me to put another bullet in Armstrong, even though another husband has already beaten me to it."

"Never mind Paul is nothing but a figment of my past. And do I need to remind you that unlike you, I have married and did my duty, even if it did turn out so very poorly. I hoped you might bring back a Russian princess or an Italian heiress to be our duchess. How boring your stories will be to endure, now that we know that is not the case," she teased, electing a chuckle from her brother.

He winked. "There were many beauties, but none that I can tell you about, Lady Victoria Worthingham. The lady you are, it would not be appropriate."

"Come, my dears. We shall have tea in my parlor upstairs," their mama said.

They headed upstairs, her brother taking in the house, seemingly remembering its beauty. It was the same for all of them when they traveled, even if just to town for several months. Dunsleigh was their home, the seat for the Dukes of

Penworth, and they adored the house and estate. It was home, no matter where their lives took them.

Victoria allowed their mama to sit beside Josh. She sat across from them, excited to hear everything he had to say. They spoke of his trip, the people he met, and those he caught up with from England while traveling. The places, sights, and countries sounded amazing, and Victoria craved to make a similar trip. Supposing she could convince Josh to help her, that was. With her mother determined to see her wed again, she did not think traveling was in her future unless it was with her husband.

The thought of Lord Melvin floated through her mind as Josh recounted his amusing and very wet details of falling off a gondola in Venice. She smiled but only half-listened as she thought of a way to bring up the invitation to Lord Melvin's home. If she were to raise it, her mama would be curious indeed and start to gain ideas she had no right to.

"We've been invited to several house parties. The first is closest, just over the border with Hampshire. Lord Melvin has invited us to stay."

Josh raised his brow, a look of confusion crossing his features. "I did not know Albert liked to host guests. Are you sure it's a house party?"

Their mama looked to Victoria, and she shrugged. "He invited us three to stay with him when you returned from abroad. That is all he said. I do not know if there will be others in attendance."

"Hmm," Josh said, a mischievous light entering his eye. "Mayhap my old friend has set his sights on my sister. A trip to Hampshire would be welcome, and I haven't seen Melvin for some time."

Victoria did not want to come across as desperate, but she also was eager to travel to his estate. If he was indeed the famous author, one whom she loved to read, well, she wanted to know for certain. To discuss his works and those that were yet to be written.

"I shall write to him this week and seek a date that is suitable for him."

Victoria couldn't help but smile at the idea. What would his lordship say when she confronted him with the page of writing? Would he deny it? The idea that it wasn't a work of his hand dampened the idea of traveling to his estate, and yet, he wasn't so very bad. Certainly not to look at. If only he wasn't so awkward and standoffish.

"Is there a reason as to why Melvin has invited us? Does he have his sights set on Victoria?" Josh asked their mama in all seriousness, his gaze slipping to Victoria in question.

She groaned, rolling her eyes. "I danced with him at our ball last week. He invited us while we waltzed. I'm sure it was merely a means of conversation, so we did not dance in silence."

Her mama studied her a moment before sitting closer to her son, taking his hand. "Oh, I am so happy all my children are back on English soil. We have missed you, Josh dear. Tell us, did you meet anyone suitable for my boy?"

A light blush stole over his cheeks before he shook his head. "No, Mama. No one to report as yet, but next year I promise to search for a duchess. Only a lady will do for the Penworth name."

"You, dear brother, are a snob, but we have missed you." The door to the room burst open, and Alice raced inside. Josh stood, pulling his sister into his arms and kissing her cheeks.

"How did you know Josh was back, my dear?" their mama queried. "I have not sent a missive yet."

Alice sat on the opposite side of Josh, squashing all three of them on the lounge. "My gardener, returning from Petworth, told me he had seen the ducal carriage travel through the town. I came as soon as I could get our carriage hitched."

Lord Arndel and their two daughters followed soon after, saying a fond welcome to Josh. The pleasant afternoon turned into a dinner and night before the fire, enjoying one another's company. Victoria reveled in the comfort of having family around, of being so fortunate to have all that she did. The idea of Lord Melvin at Rosedale, alone, without family and very few friends, left her uneasy. She did not want to feel sorry for the man, but it was so very hard not to when he was so remote, so isolated, both personally and physically.

Maybe she could entice him to be more open, more available to people. If he were the famous author Elbert Retsek, then it would only help his career if he had a more public persona.

He would benefit from her skills, she was sure of it. Now, they just had to travel there so she could begin.

CHAPTER 6

*A*lbert paced the front foyer of Rosedale, waiting to hear the sound of the Duke of Penworth's carriage. The very equipage that would bring Victoria to his estate. They had agreed to stay several days, not quite a week, and he was unabashedly excited about seeing her again.

That he would forget how to speak, how to act around her, he had decided to worry about another time. However, he looked forward to their safe arrival and seeing not only Victoria but also her brother, his good friend the duke.

"The rooms are ready for the guests, my lord," his housekeeper said, pulling his attention away from the window where he was trying to spot any carriage on the drive.

"Excellent, thank you, Mrs. Wigg." His housekeeper, pleased, nodded and started toward the back of the house.

He had planned everything for Victoria's stay, the dinners, all of which would be at least five courses. Nothing was too much for a duke's daughter. Horse rides about the estate, and boating, if she liked. His lake was one of the largest in the county, not to mention the Roman ruins that sat on an island within its center were always a location guests liked to explore.

Or would enjoy, should he ever invite any.

The sound of a carriage rumbling along the gravel pulled him back to the window, and he looked outside to see the black, highly polished carriage with the Penworth coat of arms on the door roll to a halt.

Albert looked down at his clothing, checking his attire was in order before heading outdoors. He met them at the carriage just as a footman was helping the duchess alight before the one person he seemed to be holding his breath to see once again came into view. Victoria placed her slippered foot on the carriage step, holding the footman's hand as she stepped onto the gravel drive. Her attention snapped to the house, and she looked up at it with what he hoped was pleasure before her direct, sweet gaze descended on him.

His breath caught at seeing her again and heat bloomed on his cheeks. He swallowed the unease, the fear of her rejection, and pushed past that gut-churning concern, stepping toward them all and bowing. "Your Graces, Lady Victoria, may I welcome you to Rosedale."

Victoria's mother gave him her hand, smiling. "Lord Melvin, it is lovely that you would allow us to stay here as we travel through Hampshire. We look forward to our stay, and please, call me Sarah."

Albert cleared his throat, unsure if he should follow such disregard to etiquette and forms of address that should be adhered to with a duchess. His friend, Penworth, stepped forward, shaking his hand. "Melvin, it is good to see you again. It has been too long."

Albert nodded in agreement. They had been friends since school, Eton to be exact, and as much as Penworth had tried to get him to be more outgoing, exuberant, and a charmer of anything in a silk skirt, Albert had never been able to be part of the boys' club. His nerves simply couldn't allow him to be at ease, and so eventually, he had watched his friends go off on their jaunts, and he had stayed behind. Had learned to be content with his own company.

He no longer wanted such a way of existence. He wanted a wife. He wanted Victoria if she would have him.

The woman herself materialized before him, her wide smile and bright eyes leaving him a little speechless.

"Lord Melvin, thank you for your hospitality."

"It is my pleasure," he said, turning and gesturing to the house. "Come, I have your rooms ready if you would like to freshen up. Luncheon will be served within the hour."

They made their way into the house, and he quickly took them upstairs, pointing out the rooms visible from the staircase, which were many, the library, his office that he liked to keep separate just in case of guests such as he was hosting now. The dining room, downstairs parlor, game room, and ballroom.

They made the first-floor landing, and he led them to the guest wing where two maids waited to help the duchess and Lady Victoria. Albert then led Penworth toward his room. "I hope you will be comfortable here."

Penworth glanced into his room, one of the largest and most opulent in the house, and nodded, seemingly pleased. "Of course. I'm always happy to stay with one of my oldest friends, but there is something that I do wish to discuss with you if you have a moment before lunch."

"Of course," Albert said, unable to think of what that could be, while also curious. "I shall meet you in the library whenever you're ready."

Albert did not have long to wait. Within twenty minutes, dressed in a fresh shirt and cravat, buckskin breeches, and knee-high polished boots, the duke strode into the library, his jacket idly folded over one arm.

"Rosedale is looking wonderful." Penworth walked over to the decanter of whiskey before Albert had a chance to offer him a drink, picking up the crystal decanter. "Drink?" he asked.

"It is I who should be offering you a glass, but yes, thank you."

"Do not concern yourself. I have been traveling the last year, and let me tell you, I have learned to be quite self-sufficient, which is never a bad thing, I would say."

Albert took the glass, taking a sip. "I couldn't agree more." The duke walked about the library for a few minutes before seating himself across from Albert, pinning him with his stare.

"I wanted to speak to you about the invitation that you forwarded to my family. I cannot help but ponder that there is a purpose for you doing so. Are you wanting to court my sister?"

Albert, having been taking a sip, sucked in the whiskey and choked. He coughed for several moments as he gained his equilibrium. Should he tell Penworth the truth? That he would like nothing more than to court Victoria and see if her affection for him ran deeper than mere benign fondness.

He supposed he would have to get Penworth's approval if he wished to marry his sister, so honesty was always best.

"While I have no illusions to marry Lady Victoria, I do welcome the opportunity to get to know her better. I have always liked your sister and would like to wait and see if we suit, if you agree."

Albert's stomach twisted into knots. If Penworth disagreed and did not wish him to court his sister, he was unsure what he would do. Would he go against one of the highest-placed peers in England? Would he court Victoria anyway? A rod of steel threaded up his spine, and Albert knew the answer to his own question. Yes, he would.

"We have been friends for many years, and I would welcome your suit toward her. Victoria, however," Penworth grimaced, "is of a mind never to marry again. After Armstrong, I'm sure I do not need to explain that he injured her most severely, both her heart and in society. She has grown more outspoken since the scandal, is lively, and with many hobbies. She has dogs, did you know that?"

Albert knew she had a dog, but he had assumed that it wasn't plural. "I was under the impression she had one."

Penworth chuckled, leaving his chair to pour himself another glass. He offered to Albert, and he shook his head, still drinking his first.

"She has two wolfhounds and seems to think it appropriate that both of them sleep indoors. Not to mention her horses. She has six of those. Are your stables even large enough to house her animals along with yours?"

Six horses. Two dogs. Albert felt his mouth open and close several times before a vision of her entered his mind's eye, and the numbers no longer became a concern for him. "I can always build larger stables, and as for her dogs, I can allocate a room should she wish for them to sleep indoors."

Penworth raised his brow, a wide grin lifting his lips. "Let me assure you the dogs are housetrained. Even so, what of Victoria? I would not like her to be tucked away in the country, away from town every season simply because you prefer your own company. I know we are friends, and I understand that you are not always comfortable in large crowds, but she is. You would not try to keep her here, isolated with only you for company."

"I will tolerate town if that is what she hopes for, but your assumptions are traveling a little too far ahead. I have not declared any intentions toward Victoria, and she hasn't in any way shown an interest in me in a romantic sense. I will breach the conversation with her, but not until I'm certain that there may be some hope for me."

"What will you do if she isn't looking at you with a romantic bent? Armstrong duped her before all society. Married her and fled within weeks of saying 'I do'. I fear such treatment may make others courting her difficult," the duke stated, finishing his second glass of whiskey.

"I shall be content to be her friend, as I have been, if not a very absent one." Not that Albert wanted to be such a benign gentleman to Victoria, but she was so vivacious, so different to his character, that the thought of them together even made his head spin at times.

Would they suit? That he did not know and could not say, but with her here a few days, he could gauge if there was a possibility for them. He certainly hoped that was the case.

Penworth stood, coming over to the desk and reaching out his hand. Albert shook it in turn. "Then I wish you well, my friend, and I'd be very happy should you secure my sister's affection. Victoria is a wonderful sister and will make a superb wife. You could not have picked better for yourself. Armstrong was a fool to have let her go."

Albert smiled, hope filling him at Penworth's words. Now he just needed to push down the little voice that told him he was imagining such a match and learn how to court a lady. And not just any lady, but the one for him.

Lady Victoria.

CHAPTER 7

$\mathcal{T}$he following day Victoria walked out onto the grounds of Rosedale, heading toward the lake where Lord Melvin was preparing two boats to go out on the water. The day was warm, the air fragrant, no doubt from the beautiful garden that grew off the terrace. She looked back at the house and saw that her mama was comfortably positioned on a small wrought iron chair in the shade of the wisteria, drinking tea and reading the morning's paper.

"Lord Melvin," she called out, waving to him.

He stood, waving back, and for a moment, she studied him. He was dressed in tan buckskin breeches and highly polished hessian boots. His shirt and cravat were highly starched, but the jacket seemed to make him appear casual due to his lack of a waistcoat.

Victoria had long thought him attractive, but seeing him outside of London, outside of everyone's grand home, there was something different about him. His casual appearance, his welcoming smile made her question keeping him as merely a friend. She had known him for several years, her brother's friendship with him had enabled that, but she'd never looked at him with anything but banality.

She hoped to find out if he were the famous writer Elbert Retsek. She wasn't here to try to win a husband, Paul had put paid to such absurd notions, but that did not mean there were not other things she could do. Other options open to her as a widow…

"Lady Victoria, I hope you slept well and enjoyed your breakfast."

Victoria had slept in late and had decided to break her fast in her room and had not seen anyone in the morning. "I did, thank you. The guest beds are very comfortable. I almost forgot where I was sleeping."

He smiled at her, placing two oars in the boat. "I thought we could go boating today if you wish. I have already asked your mama, and she said I might escort you over to the island."

Victoria glanced at the island, thankful it was not too far away, having never been too fond of deep water. Certainly not when attired in the dress and stays she currently wore. "You needn't ask my mama for permission. I'm a widow, my lord. Have you forgotten?"

Lord Melvin cleared his throat, a blush rising on his cheeks. "No, of course not. I was merely being polite."

She smiled, amused. "I forgive you. Now, what would you like me to do?"

"Ah," he stammered, "I shall help you into the boat if you like."

She strode over to the craft, pushing it into the water. She jumped in before it went too far off shore. "Are you coming?" she asked him. Lord Melvin chuckled, the sound gravelly and deep, and Victoria decided she liked the sound. It was warm and honest. So different from how the ton and its elite members often behaved. There had always been something about Paul's laughter that she never trusted, never thought it quite genuine.

"Right behind you, my lady," he said. He jumped into the vessel, and it wobbled precariously for a moment or two.

Victoria clutched at the sides, not wanting to particularly go for a swim, not in one of her new gowns at least. Her mother would be cross for a week if she did such a scandalous thing. Lord Melvin grinned at her, taking up the oars, and soon they were rowing across the pond toward the island.

"What is over here?" she asked, looking over her shoulder at the tree-filled island. The banks were grassed, and it looked like his lordship's gardener also kept the island grounds well-maintained.

"Roman ruins, as a matter of fact. Quite the find many years ago when my grandfather was planting the oaks. They excavated the site and decided to leave them exposed. The trees, of course, were planted around the site so as not to disturb their history.

"How wonderful. I look forward to viewing them." A few rows farther and the boat scraped along the shore, and they were docked on the island. Lord Melvin helped Victoria alight, surprising her when he swung her up in his arms, carrying her to the grassy bank.

Victoria gasped, having not expected him to do such a thing. No gentleman ever manhandled her in such a way other than her husband and he'd only touched her for six weeks before moving on to someone else. Her stomach fluttered at his sweetness.

Lord Melvin was more unpredictable than she thought him to be, but then that should not surprise her, not really. If he was indeed the gothic romance author she adored so much, then he was well-versed in how to swoop a lady off her feet, keep her from harm.

"Thank you," she said when he set her down. Her hands slid down his arms, strong and surprisingly muscular. He had masculine hands too, some fingers callused as if he held a quill for long hours. She had never particularly liked men having soft hands, they had always reminded her of dandies in London. Paul had been a dandy. She should never have married him.

She glanced back at the house and saw Josh now in conversation with her mama. "You may call me Victoria, Lord Melvin. With Mama giving you leave to call her Sarah, I see no harm in dropping titles when we're rusticating in the country."

Pleasure crossed his features before he schooled his reaction. Even so, she had seen his joy. What an odd gentleman he was, possibly one of the most intelligent and clever she knew, and yet he blushed, stumbled on his words, and shunned social events—an enigma.

"I would like if you called me Albert in return, Victoria," he said, using her given name and making her miss a beat.

She smiled and took his arm, letting him lead her into the small forest and toward the ruins. Through the trees, she could see them now. Foundations really were all that was left. A stone wall here and there, cobbled flooring, but no mosaic. What a shame the ancient tile did not survive the centuries.

"We're here." He stopped them at the side of the ruins. They were rectangular in size and large.

"The family who lived here must have been powerful. The dwelling is quite large, and no doubt there would be others still unearthed, I would assume."

"You are right. My grandfather left those buried, and you can see the trees are planted away from the ruins to keep them preserved. He did not, however, take into account the root system of the Oak tree, and we have had a little damage over the past few years."

"Well," Victoria said, stepping down into the ruins. "At least you have tried your best. That is all anyone can do."

They strode about the space for a few minutes. Victoria kneeled down and ran her hand over a stone, rubbed smooth in a circular way at its center as if it were used for grounding flour or different foods. How wonderful that such things were possible to see even now, after all this time.

"This makes me want to travel and see all the wonderful historical sites around the world." She stood, coming back to stand near Albert, who was leaning against one of the walls, content to let her explore.

"I would like to travel one day. The world is full of adventures if one is game enough to step into the unknown."

She thought about his words a moment, unsure if he really meant such a thing. He certainly didn't appear to be a person who would enjoy travel, meeting new people, the disturbance of it all. "Are you certain that is true?" She ignored his raised brow of surprise. "May I speak plainly, my lord?"

He nodded, his eyes guarded. "Please," he said.

Victoria clasped her hands before her. Could his lordship be saying everything she wanted to hear, but believing none of it? After Paul and all his lies, it was difficult to trust anyone outside of her family. Believe anyone at their word. "For the past several years, I think I could count on one hand the number of times we've seen you in town. You rarely attend events when you are in London, and this house party has a grand amount of guests equalling three. One of whom you've been friends with since you were in short coats. I cannot help but wonder," she continued, "that you're nervous when around crowds. That the London season is too much of a crush, too chaotic for you to bear. And so, I also cannot believe traveling the world would be something you would enjoy. Would I be right in that estimation?"

His mouth opened and closed several times before he said, "You're very astute, Victoria. Is my bumbling about in society so very obvious."

"Not at all. You are a most sought-after gentleman when you do attend events, even if you stumble at times. You enjoy being here at Rosedale, and I can see why you do. The house and gardens are spectacular, but to leave it all, for months on end, travel and mingle as one does abroad, I do think you would hate."

"Oh no," he argued. "I would like to travel. Who would not, but I do see why you would think that of me."

"When one gets to know you, such as I do, as little as that is, one cannot help but pick up on nuances. I want to help you if you would allow it."

"You wish to help me? In what way?"

"I'm a widow, and with that unfortunate event, it also grants me some freedom that other unmarried ladies do not have. While I have no wish to marry again, I think you would like a wife. Is that correct?"

"I have always wished to marry, to have a family, fill my home with love. You think me a foolish romantic, do you not?"

She could never think him so. If only she had married such a man as Lord Melvin and not Paul. What a disastrous mistake and one she could never repeat. "With my guidance and help, my connections, I think I could have you wed before the end of next season. Find you the perfect bride. Are you willing to allow me to train you in the art of courtship? It could also help in building your confidence so you too can travel someday."

Lord Melvin stared out at the ruins a moment, mulling over her words. His lips pulled into a pensive frown. He had lovely lips, supple and the shadow of stubble along his jaw drew the eye. Oh yes, the women would be falling at his feet, panting with want after she was finished with him.

"Very well, we have an agreement."

"Excellent, then we shall start with lessons on how to make you a rake of the first water."

He frowned. "Is it not supposed to be diamond of the first water?"

Victoria waved his words away. "Never mind that, whatever it is, we'll have you prepared for next year's season in no time. Even if you cannot find a wife, you will be more confident in crowds and open to conversation with people you have just met."

"You're only here for a few days. That will not be long enough, I fear, to help me."

"Leave that with me. I can ask for more time. If Mama thinks that I fancy you, she will want to stay. Not that I am," she reminded him, wanting the rules to be clear before they started. "Do not concern yourself. We shall have enough time."

Victoria wrapped her arm about Albert's, ready to return to Rosedale and to start their lessons. He glanced at her with a knowing look and already he appeared more roguish than she'd ever seen him before Her stomach fluttered. "Come, let us return to the house. We have much to do."

"Indeed," he drawled. "We do."

CHAPTER 8

*A*lbert waited for Victoria to meet him in the conservatory the following morning. After dinner the night before, she told him she wished to meet him in that particular room for some suggestions on making a woman more likely to swoon into his arms.

Whatever that meant.

He waited on the wrought-iron seat that sat against a matching chair and small, round table. His conservatory was aflush with flowers, scents, and even a couple of orange trees, a fruit that he enjoyed best.

The sound of slippered feet echoed out in the corridor, and he stood, bowing when Victoria entered the room.

She looked as sweet and natural as the plants surrounding them. Her soft-pink muslin gown accentuated her figure, and he wasn't without so many rakish wiles not to notice she filled her gown out in the most advantageous way. He may be a nervous, clumsy man, but he still enjoyed the sight of breasts on a woman, and Victoria had a lovely handful. He sighed. If only he would be the lucky chap to win her heart.

He'd conclude that with her helping him, it would at least

put him in close quarters to her, and maybe he could have a chance of winning her affection. Not that she saw him as anything but a clown in need of guidance to find a wife. To be more socially capable and travel without having to have his hand held.

"Good morning, Victoria." He took her hand, kissing it. She wore no gloves today, and he reveled in the softness of her skin and the sweet blush that stole over her cheeks.

"Good morning, Albert," she returned, taking back her hand and sitting down on the vacant chair at the small table he was occupied at before. "You are already showing an improvement to your gentlemanly wiles."

He joined her, throwing her an easy smile, while his innards were all a-twist. She did that to him. Made him as nervous as a virgin on her wedding night. What would she say should she know that he had never slept with a woman? He hated to think of such a reaction. Would she believe him? Or worse, laugh?

"I am trying," he replied, ready for his lesson.

"I thought this morning, while Mama is sleeping in, we could have our first lesson." She waved her hand around the conservatory. "This room not only smells divine, but it can also be a place for a tryst between couples. Not that I partook in one. Mr. Armstrong, before our marriage, was quite respectable, I must add for clarification, but the delicious scents, the beautiful outlook, the calming sound of the foun-tains, which you're lucky enough to have, all help in creating an atmosphere simply perfect for seduction."

Albert shifted on his chair, not realizing with all this talk of seduction from the very woman he'd love in his bed would make his body misbehave. Victoria certainly knew what she was speaking of and could help him. She had been married after all. Not in winning another woman, but winning her. If he found out what she liked, what made her swoon when a gentleman called, there was a chance he could court her, convince her that marriage to him would be so very different than her first.

"Go on," he urged, wanting to know more.

"If you were at a ball and happened to stroll with the woman you intend to marry, and I must stress this, you must not simply walk off to seduce anyone who takes your fancy. That will never do. I shall not like such underhanded, cruel actions toward an unmarried maid."

"I would never do such a thing," he promised, crossing his chest in the hopes that she would believe him.

She studied him a moment, her perfectly straight teeth biting her bottom lip in thought. Albert swallowed hard. Dear God, these lessons would be torture. "Very good. I'm glad you agree. Now, should you stroll into such a room, you may pick a flower, give it to the lady, tell her she is as sweet as the rose you gifted her, or whatever plant that takes your fancy."

Albert couldn't think of anyone he would rather stroll with than the woman before him. "Shall we try it now?" he suggested. "Practice makes perfect, do you not agree?"

Victoria stood, pulling him up to join her. "Oh yes, you are right."

They strolled for several steps, Victoria's arms entwined with his. "Let us pretend that you wish for me to be your wife. That we're at a ball, and you've been courting me for several weeks. Talk to me with what you think a suitor may say to the woman he adores."

Albert pushed down the nervous flutter at having to say anything romantic, especially to Victoria, whom he did, in fact, want as his own. What if she realized what he said was heartfelt? He would never get over the shame should she not want the same. Which from previous conversations, and rumor about town, she did not.

He cleared his throat. "A lovely night for a stroll. Thank you for escorting me here this evening. I know that you risk much by doing so."

She looked up at him, her eyes alight. "Hmm, very good, Albert. And I particularly liked how your voice sounded an octave lower than normal. A seductive quality that you didn't know you had, I would assume."

She would assume right. He hadn't realized he'd dropped his voice to a lower octave. "Have I mentioned how very beautiful you look this evening?" he continued, meaning every word. Even though Victoria was not adorned with jewels or an opulent silk gown, having her here at Rosedale in his arms, she was simply the most perfect lady he'd ever met.

"Thank you. You look very handsome too." She stopped and turned to face him. Victoria reached up to clasp the lapel of his jacket, her hand warm through his shirt and waistcoat.

Could she feel his heart beating madly in his chest? His mind whirled with what she was doing. Was this part of the lessons, or had his words had more effect on her than he thought they would? Shit, he did not know.

"A lady may touch you like this if you have been courting for several weeks. Even so, it would help if you did not give in to your urges. Remain the gentleman always, let the lady decide the pace of courtship."

Albert watched her lips move, but he heard very little. His body had a mind of its own, and all he could think about was kissing those sweet lips that were trying to help him.

"She may even try to lean up and kiss you. Whatever will you do then," Victoria said, leaning upon her tiptoes and placing her but a breath away from him.

His gaze dipped to her lips, and he realized he was holding her hips. "I would kiss her back."

"You could," Victoria said, stepping out of his hold, all

business and teacher-like once again. "If you had been courting and you wished her to be your wife. If not, you should excuse yourself and remove your person from the room before you're embroiled in scandal."

The idea of their lessons, of what else she would teach him, made him long for more. The scandal could go hang. He wanted her back in his arms, her sweet lips tempting his.

"Tell me what else I should know when courting a woman. I must know all the secrets if I'm to marry a woman and keep her content."

They walked on, and Victoria picked a rose, handing it to him. "This is for you," she said, "as a token of my affection. You could say something similar. But you cannot send a letter or gift, flowers only. I would suggest keeping your time alone with any lady to a minimum, even with a chaperone unless you do indeed wish to marry her."

"I'm alone with you right now without a chaperone," he couldn't help but add, wondering if she had realized such a thing.

"Oh, that does not signify. I was married and there is nothing that will shock or insult my sensibilities. I think I'm well and truly immune to anything of the sort after Paul."

Albert gave her a half smile, but inside, disappointment stabbed at him. He'd love nothing more than to kiss her, to shock her sensibilities into wanting him. Being so close to her, the desire and need she wrought was unbearable.

"You must know that for me, courting a woman is difficult. I'm not equipped with the easy manners, the words that a lot of gentlemen have when flirting with a lady. I fear all of your lessons, your help will be in vain, Victoria." Especially since he did not want any other woman on his arm but the one beside him, precious in her attempt to make him more suitable to the opposite sex.

"They will not be in vain," she said, meeting his eye. "I'm

determined to have you at your best, to show other ladies what I see in you. A lovely kind and attractive gentleman who is ready to settle into a life of domesticated bliss. A man capable and confident. I will not fail in my quest."

Albert pinned an easy smile to his lips as they walked out of the conservatory, but a weight sat atop his shoulders. He needed to figure out a way to use Victoria's lessons to his own advantage, not on others but on her.

CHAPTER 9

*L*ater that day, Victoria sat in the upstairs parlor that Lord Melvin had given her mama to use during their stay. She sat, sketching one of her wolfhounds, Pickle, from memory, but her mind kept wandering to Lord Melvin.

As much as he was interested in her lessons for him, she could not help but feel that his heart was not in it. Did he not want to marry? Or perhaps he had loved another several years ago and lost her to another gentleman. How terrible if that were the case and he was cradling a broken heart all this time, and she did not know it.

It would certainly explain the heroine in his first book, should he turn out to be Elbert Retsek, who had been grief-stricken at the death of her betrothed.

"Darling, you're scowling most severely at the parchment. Your drawing cannot be so terrible that you would glare so," her mama mentioned, catching her eye over the top of her knitting. She was making little mittens for Alice's baby due in several months.

Victoria laid the sketchpad in her lap. "You know that I'm

to help Lord Melvin be prepared to court a lady next season. He's terribly shy and awkward in social situations, and I mean to assist him with that floor. But I feel he's a little distracted. He thinks it will not work."

"While I think your motivations are honorable, do remember widow or not, to be alone with Lord Melvin during your lessons does not put you in a welcome light."

Victoria sighed, wondering when her mama would see her as a woman who had married and buried a husband. "Mama, nothing untoward will occur and I am not a virginal miss. Stop acting as though I am."

"Really, Victoria. The way you speak leaves me wondering if you had any lessons in manners at all growing up."

She grinned, knowing she often ran away whenever lessons were held. The thought of Albert flittered into her mind once more. Had she been searching for a suitable match after Paul, she may have considered him herself, but she had no desire to be anyone's property, not a second time. To trust and be so wrong with that gift was not an easy jump to make. The embarrassment she endured at Paul's affairs she had sworn never to subject herself to again. And she would not.

Not that she thought Lord Melvin would be so cruel to his wife as Paul had been. He was kind, honest, where Paul had been deceitful and ungentlemanly. A bastard through and through.

In the conservatory this morning as odd as it was, the idea of kissing him had entered her mind. He was a tall gentleman, fitted her own height well. His superfine coat tailored to perfection over his wide shoulders. His cutting cheekbones, his dark, hooded eyes that stared at her with such meaning that her heat had fluttered.

She shook the thoughts aside. He wasn't meant for her.

That was not why she was here. He was meant for someone else, someone who actually wanted a spouse.

"Have you ever considered that Lord Melvin isn't interested in any other lady? He did, in particular, invite you and your family to his estate." Her mother's knowing smile as she continued her knitting was worrisome.

Victoria frowned, having thought the invitation was due to friendship, nothing deeper than that. That they were now partaking in lessons, an idea suggested by herself, no, her mama was wrong. She shook her head, rejecting the idea. "No, he is not looking at me as a possible candidate as the future Marchioness Melvin. Do not be irrational, Mama."

"What is there to be unreasonable about? You're a duke's daughter, a sister to one. You are Lady Victoria Worthingham. There are not many men in London who would not seek such an arrangement."

"Except you forget I'm a widow to a man most of England despises since he's slept with half our acquaintances wives'. I hate that marriage is so sterile and formulaic. If I should allow a gentleman to court me again, I will only be induced into giving myself to him before God by the strongest, unbreakable love." All things that would never happen, for Victoria was determined never to allow herself to be seduced a second time into a bad match.

Her mama raised one disagreeable eyebrow. "You have been reading too many novels or listening to your sisters too much. While I wish for you all to make love matches, that is not always possible. And not all men are rakes and ravish their brides to be. You should not speak in such a way."

Victoria huffed out a breath, knowing there were no such men left in England. Her sisters had married all the best men in England.

She dismissed the thought as soon as she had it, knowing it for the falsehood it was. Lord Melvin was a good man, handsome and kind, and while he may not ravish a lady, curl her toes in her silk slippers, he certainly had the ability to, should he know what to do...

"Sorry, Mama," she said, hating to disagree with her mama. "But I'm sure you're incorrect. Lord Melvin is merely wanting company and thought to invite one of his oldest friends to his estate. Not that we'll be here long enough for me to train him in the art of courtship. We leave in under a week."

"Oh yes, that reminds me, my dear." Her mama placed down her knitting. "Your brother wants to extend it a month. Lord Hammilyn, a nearby neighbor of Lord Melvin, is having a ball, and there is a country dance at Camberley the week prior to this. Your brother wishes to attend both events, and Lord Melvin has welcomed us staying the few extra weeks."

The news could not be better, and Victoria masked the little squeal of delight at knowing they would be here and have events to attend as well. This would be the perfect time for Lord Melvin to practice all that she taught him in the art of courtship. She would have to double her efforts if she wanted to get him ready for a ball in a matter of weeks.

And, once she had his trust, and he viewed her as a close friend, as close as he viewed her brother, she would be able to ask him about his author life, should he be the man she hoped him to be.

"I'm more than happy to stay here at Rosedale, Mama. The house and grounds are beautiful. This afternoon Lord Melvin has agreed to accompany me on a ride about the estate."

"Hmm, has he, my dear." Her mama's lips pursed into another one of her *I told you so* looks before picking up her knitting once again. "Remember to take a groom with you."

Victoria stood, folding up her sketchbook and walking to

the door. "I need to change for luncheon," she said, ignoring her mother's reminder of a chaperone once again. "I shall see you downstairs presently." She left the room, shaking her head and stepped directly into the path of Lord Melvin. She careened into him, her breasts pressing up hard against this chest, sending an odd sensation directly to her stomach.

His arms wrapped around her when she would have fallen. "I beg your pardon, Lady Victoria."

She steadied herself, ignoring the feel of his hands on her back, one on her hip. Or the fact she liked the feel of his hands on her. She shook her head, stepping to the side and out of his hold. Lord Melvin was her friend, possibly her favorite author in all of England. He was not marriageable material. No gentleman was when it came to her.

"It is I who should apologize. I was not looking where I was going."

"Are you going somewhere?" he asked her, his gaze dipping to her lips.

Unable to stop herself, she licked them and spied the muscles in his jaw clench and unclench.

Oh dear. Was her mama right? Did Lord Melvin like her more than just a friend? Did he harbor feelings for her? She hoped he did not. As much as she liked him, she wasn't looking for a husband. The idea revolted her after Paul, even if her sisters seemed so incandescently happy all of the time. She had not been so lucky in love as they had been.

"I'm off to change for lunch. Are we still on for our ride this afternoon?" she asked, hoping that it was so. She had not been on a horse for several days, and it was always refreshing riding about pleasant lands such as Lord Melvin owned.

"Of course, if you still wish to."

She nodded, excited at the prospect of being free for an hour or two. "I do." He stood back, seemingly unable to think of anything else to say. Victoria smiled and stepped around him, heading toward her room. He was so very unsure of himself all the time. They would need to work on that. Why he was so she could not fathom. He had friends. She knew that because Josh had mentioned it in years past. Not that he did much with them from all accounts. He was a man with everything at his feet, and yet to Victoria, he seemed lonely. She did not like that truth. It was time he came out of the shell he had cocooned himself within and live. And she was determined to make it so.